MASTERS
360

MERLIN NORIEGA

authorHOUSE®

AuthorHouse™
1663 Liberty Drive
Bloomington, IN 47403
www.authorhouse.com
Phone: 1 (800) 839-8640

Published by AuthorHouse   02/17/2016

ISBN: 978-1-5049-7962-7 (sc)
ISBN: 978-1-5049-7961-0 (e)

You can spell the word Master on the back of the dollar bill using the letters that will connect a swastika and a cipher(360 or circle)

They were saluting with their right thumb up over their hearts me through the door windows. I was on my way out on parole. My mom came to get me from Myers Correctional Facility and drove me to her sister Veronica's apartment. Veronica Drawhorn had a two bedroom apartment at 29 Morris Street. She was on section 8. It was kind of cluttered and run down. She had a 4 year old son Frank. I slept in the bedroom with Frank on top of a bunk bed.

The first person I called was Michelle Holt. She started writing me when I was in prison. It felt good. I did like her with her blond hair and blue eyes. Her blue eyes would sparkle like white diamonds. Michelle was still 17. I told her I would wait till she turned 18 on July 23rd 92. Our first apartment was 549 Allen Street in New Britain Connecticut. Michelle was working as a receptionist at Rumo, a big insurance company. Heartford is the insurance capital of the world. We got our apartment in her name and her moms name. I paid the rent but she paid for food and other utility bills. Rent included cable and wifi. It was 950 a month on my part. It was a sweet relationship. We moved in April 1st 92

We had sex everyday. I was happy. I was in love. I know she was too. I told me all kinds of things. That my family were French Kings. They were in secret societies. They owned castles and lands and were very respected people in France. My father used to live in Brittany, in France where there was lots of rich people. And my family had their own town called Gourville. She was not only not only worked, but she was a student at Connecticut state university. She wanted to be a social worker. She was in her second semester. I gave her a thousand dollars to go shopping but she grabbed it and started ripping up the money. One night I threw about 20 grand on the queen sized bed and told her it was hers. We had sex on the bed. She told me she wasn't impressed and that I could be doing a lot better for myself. She used to ask me why Don't I go to college myself. That motivated me. One day I went to see Brother Bird at his store on park and broad. It was called Finest Communications. He sold cellular phone, laptops and assessories.

I told bird that I wanted to be a partner for a store in New Britain. I suggested we name it Daddy Glaze Wireless. He was with it, and we were off to see his lawyer. It took awhile but by Christmas 92 we opened our doors in Cousineau plaza. We were selling car alarms and stereo Systems for vehicles as well there. By that time though I had my own apartment at 44 village drive in Wetherfield Connecicutt. Me and Michelle were having Having problems living together. We were too close to eachother and i needed my space. I left new britain and lived with chance till i found My own place. Carlos Aponte had the manager at chances tell the apartment manager that i worked at chances in the kitchen. There was a place called High Hogs Resturant. We would go there often. I liked the pig snout. I recommended that Sage Allen have the chitterlings. He smelled it and said he didn't like the smell of it a place that but he gave it a try he only had a couple bits and said it was awful. It wasn't for him he said. This is where Chance would take us. Like most resturants and bars he took us to, Everything was free. He knew a lot of business people and was well known in these resturants and bars. He knew all the drug users as well. Chances is the top water hole and Merlin drinks for free in all the bars at the age of 18.

At Chances I sold a lot of drugs to college students correctional officers and cops. Once chance introduced me to the mayor. He told me that she was cool. The code for wanting an eight ball of coke was I want a shot of vodka from you. That's what she said so we met in the bathroom. Mayor Henderickow had a tan like if she went to a tanning salon. She had straight black hair in a bob hair cut. She had brown eyes. You could tell that her eye brows were painted on. She opened up the plastic bag and and dug into the coke with her fingernail. She took a sniff waited for awhile and said nice. She asked me if I told credit and I said that would be a favor for a favor. Me and Michelle had been not been seeing eachother at this time. I invited Sonias hand to my erect member inside my pants. She told me that her husband was gay. We walked out of the bathroom and were having some drinks at the bar. At the bar she had her hand on my lap. Michelle Came in. I said I had to go that was my girlfriend. She said ok. Michelle was looking at us and kinda knew if it wasn't her it would be someone else. Michelle said lets go and we left in my jeep. in the truck she said she wanted to get back together. She wanted me to come home but I said we can get back together but I was not moving back in. I was looking for my own place. We went to Star Hotel. Michelle still would come visit me. We were still a couple.

No one was selling drugs on Vernon street anymore. They moved the gate to Allen place. When I got up with the crew, Savage said he wanted to buy a kilo from me. Sage Allen never wanted to be more than a 2 and q nigga. I told him about Masters 360 but he told me he was already Nazi World and that is where he belonged. He told me he would introduce me to someone but he needed to talk to that person first. He could not even tell me the persons name. I did not even know what it was going to be about. Turned out i was meeting up with him and Stone. I recognized Stone from television. He was a reverend at inner city community church and a community activist. I did not know he was a member of something called Nazi World. Turns out he had connections in Colombia and wanted to work with Sage Merlin. Sage Allen said that is the nigga Merlin. Charles Nicolas De Gourville has a business named taxus where he would boost fraudulantt income tax returns for his clients and take his cut. Jason Mendez was baracaded in a stolen Buick Croix and would not comply with swat team police officers Masters 360 and Nazi World are cousin organizations that were formed in Connecticut prisons. Masters 360 incorporated a lot of Nazi material

Allen used to bag up half of grams of cocaine and sell it for 50 and he would only break a rock for no less than $20. Allen had blue eyes and blond hair he was a member of nazi world and many referred to him with his title sage. Heartford police arrived at the streets of Newberry and Preston to a dead John Shane who was ejected from his motorcycle in Heartford 8:07 am Merlin is handcuffed by police because they said he was interfering with a police office because he said he didn't know anything about An accident. He was escorted by Wethersfield police to the Heartford police department. While taking merlin to the police department. He says "All we got is us, you never lived my lifestyle never seen a brick never seen a penthouse. Its all love in the heart of heartford"

Sage Allen just hit this guy in the face for yelling at him. He says it is not a safe situation when people invade your personal. Allen Holt fights too much so I told Micheal Ssavage I needed help getting my jeep fixed and he told the police I was at his apt that, morming. So Sage Allen shot that nigga. the last time I saw Micheal he was in a police cruiser outside my apartment building. the next thing I know word on the street was he died. I got it made. people from the Dominican republic love me I remember the first time I sold cocaine to a state trooper. I was introduced to him through my uncle and I sold him 1 gram for $100 I am very fortunate to be making approximately a million a week for basically doing nothing. but there are bigger niggas than me.

Stone for instance must be making millions of day of real estate, fast cars and drug money. he is the leader for Nazi world. I can honestly say Stone helped rebuild the city of Heartford Connecticut. Sage Allen don't do shit but get in trouble. Spoiled brat

Colombia to Dominican Republic to Connecticut just ask all the addicts where the money went. Heartford is the cocaine capitol of connecticut. I remember trading 2 kilos of coke for 50lbs of bubba kush and having a free weed party at Tom Alton's penthouse apartment. You can get a kilo of coke in heartford for 18 thousand dollars if you know the right people. nah I don't sale crack but the coke is similar. I sniffed cocaine once, herion one night, crystal meth once, and smoke weed a few time and im not addicted to nothing but the money Heartford is the cocaine capitol of connecticut. I believe in reincarnation and that we are living in hell when we get kicked out of heaven. Where is god?

Allen Holt's father was drafted in the army during vietnam

One day Sage Allen had to jump on his fathers back to help defend his mother whom was being beat by his father. Sage merlin was in a gifted and talented program in the fifth and sixtg grades. He was often picked on by other students throughout school

Sage Allen had to defend himself against other students in school. He was the target of violence often in school Sage Allen as singled out by his sixth grade teacher Ms Jackson. He got in trouble at home because he got bad report card all year long Sage Allen's mother argued with Ms Jackson and was about to fight with her when sage Allen's final report card came home with good grades The grades on sage Allen's final report card in the sixth grade were changed from earlier report cards that year. He graduated elementary. I left home when i was 15 because i got a dirty urine testing for cocaine because i first would put numb my mouth to see if was good. I first started selling cocaine at the age of 15 because my mom wouldnt let me work because i was getting bad grades in high school

My first night selling drugs was on a Friday night. I had $100 and bought an eight ball(3 1/2 grams). I was on the corner of Adam and Albany From the eight ball i made $400 after being up all night(an all nighter) There was no one else selling drugs on the block that night except for lace who was further down the one way street

The nickname i was going by was Daddy Glaze. That morning heck, Steve, and ghost came and me and lace went to breakfast with them at Hernando Resturant. After breakfast, lace went home and the rest of us returned to 121 Adam Street. Mack was a fat white nigga, and he was taller than me. He started wrestling with me but he was weaker than me. I threw him on a parked car. While I was holding Mack on the parked cars front end his cousin from New York came up put his hand in my pocket snatching my $400 and ran. Heck was gone with my $400 and when i returned to the block everyone was gone. I then went to body's apartment on baltimore street. I really liked working. I was a cashier. I learned to count cash fast and i would move customers through the checkout in a hurry. I told body what happened. I didnt have any money so i didnt return to tge block anymore. I ended up getting my job back at Frazine Grocery

One of my managers would let me work more than 40 hrs. Larry evans was his name. I bought myself a stainless steel watch and a stainless steel bracelet that had diamonds in it. I even had a female co worker that was 19 approach me and got with me as my girl.

One night after work i missed the bus so i walked home to my grandmothers apartment. I decided to walk down adam streett. I saw Steve and he was like whats up? He was talking kind of loud and asking me why i wasn't around. He said his uncle was a cop and Said that i snitched on rondell lampley abour raping some prostitute. I never even heard about it until that night because lampley wasn't in my circle. About 8 white niggas beat me up and took my watch and bracelet. My upper lip was busted as i got punched in the face. Lonnie edwards was the one who held me in a head lock as i got punched. He let me go. I dont know why. To be honest i dont know where steve. I ran as fast as i could after lonnie let me go. I ran towards the train tracks. I heard steve calling my name running towards me. I guess he Didn't know where i went because he didn't follow me. I walked down the railroad tracks cut up through blue hills ave and walked. Jefferson park till i made it home at 2628 main street. I had an uncle who was a year older than me named heavy. He asked what happened to me and I told him the puerto ricans got me. The puerto ricans were beefing with the whites in those days and I grew up in a white Neighborhood event hough i was half trinidadian and cherokee. All the whites knew my dad richard noriega

I kept going to work but one day i didnt know i was scheduled to work. I went to pick up my check later that day and found out i lost my job. I went with my heavy on enfield street. They were all kids my age that i remembered from aden miller elementary school

These white kids where ballers. They had lots of stainless steel jewelry and they had volvos, mercedez, and all the other luxury vehicles. Later that night i decided to buy a quarter ounce of cocaine from one of the guys in a volvo that my uncle told me about. Jazzy was his name. It was alot of competition on the block so i didnt even come close to making my cash back. I dont remember if i doubled my money cause I Was always spending money. Food clothes and i would give my grandmother a little something. One night I got in a rental car with Smash, fast eddie. And Junebug from enfield street. We rode to park street and fast eddie pulled out the 357 on the puerto ricans. He was in the front passenger seat and I was sitting right behind him. He took a couple of shots toward the ground. It was cold that night and snow was on the ground around park and putnam. I heard Lupe got shot in the but and had to go to the hospital. Smash put his foot to the metal and we took off.

Well enfield street lasted about 7 months. I landed a job at vivada resturant. i worked the buffet and would prep food for the buffet. I worked at vivada restaurant for about 9 months. New mangement came in and laid me off due to slow business. I didnt go back to selling drugs because alot of guys were going to prison and getting double digits in court. My cherokee uncle, heavy, Had landed himself in prison at the age of 16. He shot and killed a guy but because everyone said the victim was a cocaine addict who

Tried to rob heavy with a knife. Its just that heavy pulled out the 9 mili beretta. I was on the bus coming home from Witney mall. I was there since school let out pretty much till around 9 pm filling out job applications. Sage Allen was on the back of the bus. I recognised him from school and had known that he got shot while i was in juvinile detention for a month I got caught with 3 ounces of cocaine. I nodded my head to them. He was with savage who i also recognised. I was getting off the bus in front of the Wellings insurance building. There was another kid from my old high school on the bus. He had a stainless steel gucci link. It really caught my eye but i guess i Really caught Sage Allen's eye. He grabbed the guy and snatched the chain and ran. We all started running with sage Allen. we went around the corner behind town hall and waited for awhile. We ended up going to sage Allen's apt and his mom was in florida with his sister so we were there for days. It was the fourth of july 90. That was the first time i ever drank alcohol. We had a bottle of grey goose vodka. I didn't drink much but i think sage merlin was drunk. Some girls were talking to me and sage merlin and gave us their numbers. We saved their number in our cell phones Crazy nigga, Sage Allen tried to snatch some glow in the dark necklaces a lady was selling. We went down the street. These puerto ricans that. Hung out with were smashing cars and people would look at them from inside their locked cars. I even heard car doors lock. I thought it was Us having fun. Sage Allen must of caught a lot of attention that night and i guess so did i. Some of his friends from park street wanted to Wanted to fight me. Sage Allen stood up for me and said that i was down with them now. I lived with sage Allen and his mom for about two Years. Gonboy brought me over to washington and broad. Where we became partners. He had 7 grams but he didnt know how to count. So i sold it I made almost 600 of the quater and gave gonboy 300 we got in the cadilac with his cousin where he got the 7 grams. He bought another 7grams. I was 16 and never seen anyone sniff coke before. Gonboy was a little older than us. Around 22. Seeing him get high as a friend was new to me. I didnt want to be his partner any more so i kind of avoided him after that. I didn't think you could use and sell at the same time. I didnt sell drugs again until i found a job at steins department store. I worked in the shoe department for two weeks. I didnt have my Social security card so i lost my job. She told me i had two weeks to get it but i really didnt know how to obtain it. It was oct. 90

Of my cousins from the north end that hung on burton street. He said he let me owe him $20 so i had a deal. Jack Hunt was a good guy And everything but his number got called when he got caught throwing nine ounces of cocaine out of the window of his car while being chased. By east heartford police department. Around december i was buying a solid ounce and saving up cash. I had about 5 grand saved up. The puerto ricans knew i was making money but one of sage merlin's niggas got kinda jealous and was looking for someone that would rob me with Him. Sage Allen was always sticking his neck out for me. i needed a cocaine connection and Sage Allen introduced me to an older dominican guy. Me and Mega talked in his Toyota camry in front of Sage Allen's moms building at 95 Allen Place. Mega told me the smallest he sold was 2 and quarter ounces at a time. I didnt really want to invest in that much coke but this was the best connection i had ever had and this had to work Out. I moved down to vernon and broad street and started selling drugs to the prostitutes. Tish was my first fish with her pimp kelli.. She had an older red convertable cadilac that her mom had left to her when she past away. Her and kelli used to shoot up cocaine and heroine. One night tish got pulled and went to jail and kelli begged me to help with the money to get her out. I think i gave him 50 which was 10 % to the court in wetherfield superior court. When she got out it was like we were new friends. She would run customers to me and let me drive her car. I was paying $1,300 for two ounces and a quarter ounce and i was selling it for

no less than 100 a gram. I would not even sell it. Sell it
to someone if they had 19 dollars. A twenty piece was the
least money i would accept. I would not cut the coke from
mega but I was breaking up the big chunks of compressed
cocaine into smaller chunks around the size of a gram or
half of gram. I would bag the Grams off a scale into plastic
sandwich bags. I was making about 15,000 a week till i
got arrested for two ounces and twelve hundred dollars.

In the beginning of April. I originally got arrested
with a half of gram in my bald up fist. The detective
found keys to my safe in my pocket. He asked me wherw
i lived and i gave him my grandmothers address on main
street. He went back to the building where i had came
out came shelly with detective hodste. She walked over to
Allen place with the detective. I am told they went up to
the 34 th floor and told Mrs. holt that they would arrest
her too if she didnt cooperate. She gave them the safe but
she said she didnt know what was in it. I remember now.
I waa charged with possesion of a drug factory. A scale
was in the safe as well as sandwich bags and the cocaine
and $1,200. Me and my mom were getting along i was
saving cash with her and buying her things so she bonded
me out with my cash. My bond was $20,000. She gave
simpson and simpson bailbonds $2000 to get me out but
it took 10 days because she wanted me to sit in jail and
think about it for. It for a little while. I did. When i came

out i bought a kilo from mega for 18,000 I started letting people owe me cash. I would give them cocaine and wait. I was charging drug dealer 800 an ounce. Not selling grams anymore. I would sell eightballs for 100 and up. It depended on who the person was.

Sage Alen started introducing me to more people. He was weeding out the good street kids to be in my circle. thats how i met hardcore And his father chance. Chance would let us sell to people in his bar Chances. I was moving about 3 kilos a week to drug addicts and drug dealers when i was 17 years old. Around august i bought my first car a audi 4000. I remember saving $30,000 a week in those last months of the year and i got caught with a half ounce in november 91. This guy greg was drunk At chances he wanted me to sell him an eightball so we got in his buick verano. He was swerving all over the road. I told him to pull over. I ended up driving him home and he told me i could take his car. I didnt hear from next day and the car had a flat tire. I replaced the tire. I was still driving his car and i had a half ounce sell in west heartford. When i was almost to the location i was pulled over buy a cop car. I pulled up into a parking lot and thought maybe he would just let me walk because i didnt do anything wrong. Oh my god, the car was reported Stolen. I think monster snitched on me because before the cop put me in the cop car he put his hands down my pants and felt the half ounce. In my briefs. I told him my briefs were calvin klien but he didnt find that amusing. Greg came to court the next morning and said he did not want to press charges. I ended up saying that i had a drug problem and was given a year for possesion in west heartford court. I stayed in and was convicted for my earlier drug case in heartford court. All other chareges Were dismissed. I got 5 years probation in heartford running concurrent with the 1 year in west heartford. I did a total of 30 days and was Put out on parole. I was under the 10 persent law for non violent offenders. I turned 18 December 10. 91 in mycrs youth correctional institute.

I went to narcotic anonymous, alcoholic anonymous, second chance programs and catholic church. The first sunday after my birthday the puerto ricans told me i was a master I asked Rivera what they was taking about. Pedro was like come on bro you with us or not? We all Masters 360. Thats our organization for handling our business in the streets. our business is drugs and prostitution. I was like for real guys and scott said im italian and im all In. I've been down since. No questions asked. They never told me i had to do anything. I used to work at finest communications from the day i got out of myers youth institution on parole. I had to see my parole officer three times a week instead of five days a week because i had a job. I would hang there when i wasn't Working. I met a lot of drug dealers through finest communications. It became a major drug point in heartford. They would put the drug money. In the safe in the back room till i arrived with the coke. He was an easy business man. I would charge him 18,000$ per kilo and he would Sell it for $20,000. He made an easy $2000 per kilo. Charles Nicolas De Gourville had a very nice boat in New York we used to use and he own Castle De Gourville a luxury apt building on Gourville Circle in Brooklyn New York. We used to have the best parties with Charles. One time they had a rapper name infinite. Masters of the universe will always be paid we take the weakest rules and make them better remember we come in for the win and begin to master over and over again. Infinite minded I just signed in looking for a style like mines they wont find shit. I am the professonal they are the audience. This morning Allen was driving my grey jeep Laredo speeding past a stop sign and crashed a green kawasaki ninja motorcycle which flipped over. The rider of the motorcycle was ejected from his bike into the air and landed on the sidewalk. Merlin restarted the jeep and fled the scene. The driver of a Lexus behind him wrote down the licence plate of the jeep. Allen drove the dented jeep back to Merlins's building Allen went to talk to Merlin about the hit and run with Merlin's jeep Laredo. Merlin told Sage Allen that he would handle it.

On marzo 3rd 93 i woke up to wethersfield and heartford police officers at my door questioning me about a motor vehicle accident. They asked if they could come in and i said sure. Thet questioned me as i sat on my sofa in the living room. I told them i didnt know anything About an accident. They asked me if anyone had key to my jeep and i told them my girlfriend did. They asked to check my pants pocket For weapons and pulled out my key chain. They asked whose keys were on the kitchen counter and i said my girlfriends. They then told me i was Under arrest for interfering with a police officer. I said okay and they put handcuffs on me behind my back. On the way out they looked in Michelle's leather coat which was on the dinning room chair. They pulled out her drivers license and asked if it was my girlfriend in Photo. I said yeah. They escorted me downstaira and in the front parking lot all the doors hood and trunk were open wide for my jeep laredo. Officer rig authorized a protective sweep of my apartment and they found a half of kilo in a coat pocket in the bedroom walk in closet. I saw savage get placed in the back of a police cruiser but he was driven off after me. When i got to heartford police headquarters they said That i was not under arrest and that they just want me for questioning. They came to my apt about 11:45am and held me in an interogation Till about 5:00pm. All they ever asked me "do you know anything about drugs and guns in your apartment. I told them no. They later released me About the same time they got their warrent around 5 pm. But detectives in their warrant said that i went with them willingly to the police. Department to answer questions which was false information put in their warrant. They also said that i said both sets of keys belonged to my Girlfriend when i never said that. They gave information to savage and he cooperated with the police. He only said i was at his apartment that morning cause the police said I was at his apartment and they know it. So he agreed to get out of there becauase he was on probation and didnt want any problems. He did not include that in his statement but he did say that i asked for help to get my jeep fixed. Their warrant did not mention a protective sweep but they were looking for motor vehicle stuff. They said they found the drugs after the warrant. Under arrest for interfering with a police officer. I said okay and they put handcuffs on me behind my back. On the way out they looked in Pockets to michelles leather coat which was on the dinning room chair. They pulled out her drivers license and asked if it was my girlfriend in photo. I said yeah. They escorted me downstaira and in the front parking lot all the doors hood and trunk were open wide for my jeep Laredo. Officer Smith authorized a protective sweep of my apartment and they found a half of kilo in a coat pocket in the bedroom walk in closet forgot about the kilo in my apartment. that's A SMALL THING TO A GIANT. I PUT SO MUCH STUFF IN SO MANY PLACES. POLICE ARE DIRTY THO. U OPEN THE DOOR FOR THEM AND THEY LIE CHEAT AND TRY TO GET YOU TO COOPERATE. I WOULDNT GO TO NO POLICE DEPARTMENT FOR QUESTIONING. THAT WAS AGAINST MY WILL. I saw savage get placed in the back of a police cruiser but he was driven off after me. When i got to heartford police headquarters i was That i was not under arrest and that they just want me for questioning. They came to my apt about 11:45am and held me in an interogation

Till about 5:00pm. All they ever asked me "do you know anything about drugs and guns in your apartment. I told them no. They later released

They asked if they could come in and i said sure. Thet questioned me as i sat on my sofa in the living room. I told them i didnt know About an accident. They asked me if anyone had key to my jeep and i told them mt girlfiend did. They asked to check my pants pocket For weapons and pulled out my key chain. Thet asked whose keys were on the kitchen counter and i said my girlfriends. They told me I was About the time they got their warrent around 5 pm. But detectives in their warrant said that i went with them willingly to the police Department to answer questions which was false information put in their warrant. They also said that i said both sets of keys belonged to my Girlfriend when i never said that. They gave information to savage and he cooperated with the police. He only said i was at his apartment that morning cause the police said iI was at his apartment and they know it. So he agreed to get out of there becauase he was on probation and didnt want any problems. He Did not include that in his statement but he did say that i asked for help to get my jeep fixed. There warrant did not mention a protective sweep but they were looking for motor vehicle stuff. They said the found the drugs after the Warrant where wethersfield detectives applied for their own warrant and found another half kilo and $10,000. In a closet off the patio. On marzo 8 th i was arrested coming out of my apartment at 44 village drive apartment 305. On an arrest warrant with a 750.000 cash bond. Wethersfield detectives questioned me at the wetherfield police department and asked me if I knew anything about drugs or a motor vehicle fatal hit and rub and I kept saying no. They then put me in a holding cell all by myself

The wethersfield detectives also asked me if michelle was driving my jeep i told them it had problems and she didnt drive it she had her own. I was moving 100 kilos of cocaine a week easy. I paid 9 grand a kilo and sold it for atleast 18 grand a kilo. I put it out there at 80% pure.

My mothers maiden name is natasha Drawhorn. She is a native scrooger from the cherokee tribe.

I once met diana cousineau of framing concepts. She was a talented artist. She showed me some artwork for the walls in our offices At daddy glaze wireless. I heard it was her father paul who was the architect and owner of cousineau plaza. She was a very attractive woman for 39 years old. She was tall and well proportioned. She had black curly hair and blue eyes.

Diana looked at us and spoke to us like she wanted to be our sweet adoptive mother

Inner city faith community church is the name of a church where reverend palvo works out of. He was about five foot 3 skinny. Sky blue eyes and light blond hair. He was 35 years old. Drove a Porshe 111. When i got to court on marzo 9th 93 Michelle paid 200$ for my attorney to represent me for arraignment. Julio Rodriguez had my bond reduced to 400,000$ cash bond and got my case tranfsered to heartford superior court and out of wethersfield superior court even though the prosecutor Asked for a million dollar bond. I could hear someone saying oh my god when he asked for this. I also heard Michelle in the background crying. After court i was put in an ice cream truck and sent to heartford county jail. I waa directed to east 14 cell 35. An officer locked in a Room slid a door to his face and asked me my name. I told him and then the hispanic guard asked me what i was in for. I told him drugs and I Smiled. He directed me to 35 cell. It was a single cell. I appreciated living alone. Michelle sent me $1500. I bought a television and radio and Went to commisary every week spending 50 dollars. In two weeks time I was booked for vehicular homicide, and evading a responsibility. Allens, brother birds and my lawyers came to visit me in the first three weeks of my time

In the county. The best deal i was getting was birds lawyer saying i would probably get out of prison when i was 40. Didnt look good for me The war between the lord kings and the masters started because divine was fucking a masters girl. kevin hines did not play that shit. when he found stacy in bed with divine he was heated. kevin thew a flashlight that was on the bedroom dresser at divine. he told divine to get up out of the bed. divine was crown for the lord kings he got on the horn for his brothers to come pick him up. he was in a hurry to get out of stacy's apartment. the sex was not worth drama'. kevin got close and slapped the phone out of his hands. the call was incomplete. "what are you going to do nigga?" said kevin. "come on man" divine replied. he was trying to walk by kevin but kenvi attacked him. he left with a swollen eye. he went straight to to stylez hair salon which was a lord kings hang out spot. he reported the incident to his fellow brothers and they said '' mission time. they went back to the apartment, kicked down the door and shot kevin in who was standing in the hallway to the front door. they left and disappered in the columbus 99 truck. after that i heard divine was in puerto rico with his own army of lord kings. they started putting in work with the columbians. divine was soon having cocaine shipped all around the u.s. he was wanted was never a suspect by the police for killing kevin but he was a wanted man with the masters." i dont know much about divine. never really met him. i didnt understand why nigga mess with other niggas girls. he had had a long run. eventually the columbians killed him for owing them for 5000 kilos. i heard it was garbage coke but they wanted their money anyway. divine was not going to pay for it and he suffered the consequences. they cut him up real bad, i heard, they stabbed him him i the gut several times and then cut his neck. i was still in prison at the time but i read the puerto rican newspaper in my cell. it was pretty graphic showing everything. i couldnt make out evverything in the paper but in the article you could see him laying in his blood. he had a short run from 94 till 97. all because of a girl, niggas were dying in connecticut and other niggas were getting long prison terms for murdering them. I mostly did not come out of my cell except for breakfast and hamburger day or to use the phone in the tier every morning from 8-10 am. I would get off the phone if someone asked for it but that rarely occured. The only problems that i had in the county was with the Guards. One of them wrote me up for washing my clothes in a trash bag in the tiers trash can. We all washed our clothes this way because Laundry exchange was only for tans and they sold tide on commissay. He wrote me up and i asked to go speak to him. He slid the door to his face open and i threw threw the displinary report at his face. He slid the door closed and told me to go to my cell. That afternoon another report was slid under my door for assault on an officer. My other displinary report was also for assault on an officer. It was our recreational period and i started banging on my door because The officer would not open my door. He called for assistance saying i was. Creating a disturbance. I was being escorted to segregation. The other officers opened the staff bubble to collect the displinary report and i threw a lit cigarette to his chest. one Chinese kid was there for trying to kill his mother in her sleep. him and one of his friends were trying to collect her insurance money. I think he was 20. He and his friend was high on crystal meth at the time. the Chinese kid said he would give me two for one on a noodle soup. I gave him a soup but on commissary day he did not pay me before breakfast one day I grabbed him by the neck and held him against the table saying wheres my bill. another inmate broke it up but I didn't get in any trouble for it. other than that the county was smooth sailing. I used to go to court about once every three weeks mostly continuance. There was a supreesion hearing where all of the cops testified in my case. my public defender was trying to say that the drugs were illegaly obtained violating my fourth admendmant rights. I had to testify that it was my apartment and my version of what happened on marzo 3rd. my motion to suppress evidence was denied. and I pled no contest and received a 15 year sentence with a right to appeal the judges decision. the prosecutor in heartford superior court part a was suggesting a 25 year prison. term other than a trial case where he wanted to give me 70 years. I was sentenced on September 27th 93 and was transfered to cogosti reception and special management center in latimorre Connecticut. I was assessed for educational; and vocational purposed. giving a physical saW mental health and dental. I asked mental health for something to sleep because I couldn't sleep at night. I was mostly up all night in my cell watching television. and sleeping during the day in the county they said they didn't offer anything to sleep. they was a guy from charter oak housing project there who recognized me from allen place at college pizza. and there was a guy there from Washington and broad street who was representing lord kings hard. i never went to masters 360 meetings and kind of did my own thing me Joey from charter oak and cholo sat together for our meals and hung out tighter at recreation. joey had a drug charge and cholo had a gun charge and was on the news for being a violent gan member, they should pictures of him with guns on the news and he was doing 9 years joey had a year but was a good joker who liked talking about girls. we knew some of the same girls. one day the lord kings told cholo he had to do a mission. he did it. he walked toward this huge whitew guy and punched him on the side of his head. the guy was backing up and fell. the correctional officers were quick as if they knew what was going to happen. they broke it up and took cholo to segregation. I was tranfered back to heartord county jail to sign some paper work for my appeal with my public defender and then sent to ellsworth correctional center. This was the joint know as big ells. I went through the all purpose room and was removed from my street clothes. They asked where I wanted to have my posseions(that I couldn't have in the facility) sent to or if I want to discard or donate them. I donated them. I was placed on 19 galley cell 46. the prison was 50 stories tall as most government buildings were in Connecticut. I mostly stayed in my cell except for chow call. the showers were nasty so I would soap up and rinse in my single cell. there was a lord king named scope who

I would play chess with from cell to cell. We had numbered our chess boards with the number 1-64. we would be up all night, calling numbers. there was a guy who knew my uncle. he was from enfeild street and he recognized me. he wanted to know what I was doing in prison and I showed him my newpaper article. he disappeared I didn't know whast happended to him. I just assumed that he was assigned to another part of the prison. I was assigned to 19 galley as a tierman whose duties where to sweep and mop the teir but the officers never let me out of the cell to work. I was paid 17.50 a week and didn't say antything i went to classification and was assigned to kitchen detail. i was moved to north block 5 and was fitting in ok. i would play spades with Hispanics. my celly was a Dominican guy who was cool and he also had 15 years for drug charges. one day the guy from enfield street moved in the unit and was in a cell all by himself. he asked if i would move in the cell with him before they put someone in the cell with him that he was going to have problems with. since he was from heartford i did move in the cell with him. he didn't have much but he was working in the kitchen as well. he didn't have a television but i shared mine. he was in prison doing a 17 year prison term for shooting and paralyzing ANOTHER TEENAGER. he was 18 his name was trevon Santo. he showed me pics of his victim hanging out with some other guys. it happended because the victim stole a fiend from from him when he went to go get his stash. he ended up going to get his gun and came back and shot the other hustler. he used to want to wrestle and play physical games. one morning he ripped my sheets off me and told me to get my lazy ass up. i was on a budget and used to share my 10 a week commisay with http://him.one night we were in line to take showers. we kind of stuck together. recreation was over with but we didn't make it to the showers. we heard the annoucement to lock down but i followed my celly into the shower anyway. one of the coorectional officers came over and said didn't you bitches hear me. i was receiving military traiining in the mail at the time and was ready for anything i thought. i told the officer if he though i was a bitch he could come in the shower and fight with me. he told me nah he didn't want to fight. i turned around to walk away and the officer punched me in the mouth

i felt burning and when i went to lick my lip i could taste the blood that was coming out of my upper lip. I turned back around to face the correctional officer to see what was going on and he was running in reverse. Travon was walking up on him and questioning him why did you do that to him he yelled. i was then grabbed by a really big guard who was mostly fat. officer penbrook and staff was there fast becuas the officer jones who hit me had pressed his panic button before he hit me they escorted me and trev as I called him to segration on south 87. they put trev in the shower and put me in the rec area with several other inmates. one of my brothers boogy was there and asked me what happened to me because he thought I was keeping a low profile. I told him and he said dam you let a white guy nigga you. I was pulled out one day and the lutinent asked me to sign a statement on my version of what happed. I was later charged with assault on an officer at the d.r. board given outside charges. I was found guilty at the d.r. board even though there was several statements in my behalf from other inmates saying the officer hit me. the state trooper came to see me officer jones had been to the hospital because he got a cut on his hand. he said that I hit him. funny how things work. I was sent to the special managent center and was going to court. someone else from seg was there AND HE JUST TOLD EVERYONE MY BUSINESS threw the ventsI was told that officer jones was actually born neil gooch who was a drug dealer turned informant to the feds in new haven ct. he got with 6 kilos and ended up ratting on his friends changed his name and became a guard.

I was in a cell by myself for phase one of the special managent program going to court. even my public defender knew about offeicer jones and his history but he got me 1 year concurrent with my sentence for third degree assault. he said I could beat the system so I plead under the Alfred doctorine. I told the judge what happened and she just ignored my side of the story and said an officer could defend himself

I used to play chess thu the vents in special managent with ribbit and Osborn. two guys from new haven. they used to appear cool. I was classified and told I was going to phase 2 and would get my television back. upon leaving ribbit told me to watch out for king bubba going to phase 2 was a mistake. I was being played. I was put in the cell with one of my brothers who was often testing me. he used to tell about other gangs members from out of town. he was from heartford. he was placed there for his non involvement in a RIOT BUT the department gave him and others charges because they did not follow instructions and follow the guards. he used to put his hands on me and say he was playing. if he wasn't short to discharging maybe he was a bubba. I used to start thinking that everyone was snitching. when he left to go phase three I was the only master on the unit. no one disrespected me and everything was cool between me and the other inmates. I thought. I went to phase three and there was an old Hispanic guy on the bottom buck when I was coming back from court. the guard told him he was assigned to the top bunk. he said he had a bad back. I shouldnty have said anything because I know guys ar3 conners. but I did I said have the bottom bunk. they officer said he would change the assignment. one day a guard brought me five bags of coffee from white. the guard said he knew my whole family but I didn't know him officer morales when the guard left my celly said stop snitching. I was the only master in this unit as well. he was with heartbreakers another Puerto rican gang in hearford. there was this other guy from the county I remember now. he was a white guy from the avenue who tried to test me with tramp was on the low calling me a snitch. he tested me because I knew the truth about him in the streets. he was one of those guys trying to keep the north vs the south end street wars but he was buying drugs from one of my brother named rundown

I don't know whT MY OLD CELLY WAS SAYING WITH HIS BROTHERS BUT I NOTICED THEM TALKING TO A CORRECTIONAL OFFICER. when it was lockdown time

he stayed outsiden the cell door. when the officer told him to lockdown he no this mutherfucker is going to kill me. they put both of us back and phase 2. there was no more special management programs being held at the facility. a new facility was opening up called the supermax. Kurtz coorectional facitlity was a 500 million dollar project. it was a state of the art facility. no wonder our nation was broke.

Segragation. Officer ken jones went to the hospital for a cut on his fist. The state troopers went to the hospital to investigate the matter

Officer jones told them that i assaulted him and there was an altercation. He filed charges against me. I was also found guilty in dr court For assault on an officer, threats and gang affiliation because they said they had a letter saying i was a master in my cell

I went to my groups in the supermax but when i was almost back in population a captain pulled me into the office saying he didnt think it Was a good idea if he let me back into population. He said he was sending me to a close monitering unit for gang members. What was i Supposed to say. I told him thats a big weight around his neck. I was then escorted back to my cell by the a few officers.

A week passed by and i was sent back to ellsworth. It was night time when i arrived to my cell. I had a cellmate and i thought i recognized Him from somewhere. He said he didnt know me but he was nosey. tge next morning on the way back from breakfast i could hear him telling a guy

I was his brother and that he knew me from new haven county jail. Another guy yelled out that he saw me in the supermax

Carl macaley was a strange fellow. He was always in the cell saying he was god and he would contantly start fights with me. He was muscular 2h2 hours ago

But i was taller and stronger. I only weighted about 186 but i was doing 1000 pushups on mondays wednesdays and fridays. Sets of 100

There were alot of whispers. I over heard one of my brothers magnificent telling the captain to move me in his cell. The captain said no.

I heard a guy telling me under his breath that he could help me. Loco was the grand master. He had an idea. Angel González was acting up. I dont know what he was doing but he had to be bounced. Loco sent vanilla to watch and me to bounce him. I never bounced anyone before It waa for two minutes. Angel was from waterbury. After that angel and another brother from waterbury would show their true sides to me

Angel was always putting his hands on me but i would push him aside. He was still trying tho. One day his boy from waterbury brought me up Charges to a supreme master. He said i threatened him. The supreme master known as intelligent ordered me to be bounced for two minutes.

Vanilla came to my cell and gave me the word. Wiz was the guy who said i threatened him and he timed it. Angel and vanilla bounced me for 1 Minute. A bounce is normally by one person punching you on your physical. After that vanilla said go talk to intelligent. I did. I asked him why i had to be bounced and he gave me his expanation. I told him i didnt threaten any brother. He asked me where i was from and i told him Heartford. He told me to go talk to loco. Loco told me to bounce that brother for lying on me. He told me to break his jaw

I guess word got out about wiz because he was tranfered the next morning before he could get his bounce

Wiz was vanillas cellmate but they werent getting along. After wiz got transfered vanilla had me moved in the cell with him. Vanilla was from heartford too. We got along reql good. Angel was shaping up now that wiz was gone. One day he asked to borrow my rock n roll magazine.

I let him see it but when he gave it back a page was missing. Vanilla asked him wht he stealling from me when all he had to do was ask for it. He started laughing. The next morning i went in his cell. He was brushing his teeth in the back of the cell. I decided to take One of his dove soaps. I put it in my cell and told vanilla to hold it down. I was on my way to the outside recreation when i heard angel saying pop 24. I ran back to my cell. And angel was starting to walk in my cell. I pushed him from behind and he landed against the desk

That was in the back of the cell. Vanilla held the back of his head and mushed his face against the desk and told him to get the fuck out.

Vanilla graduated the close monitering program. I was there for a total 6 months going to groups and stuff but when interviewed by the Captain he said he wanted me to spend another 6 months in close monitering. Me and vanilla normally did push ups together on the tier.

Intelligent must of thought it was good for us and ordered that all master worked out for 20 minutes on the unit together with fellow masters. Angel didnt want to work out with us. When challeging intelligent he was going to lose. Intelligent sent an order to loco and loco laid it down to me. He told me to cut angel in his face because they had enough of him. He has to get terminated which we call a t

I didnt cut him in the face. I took two other brothers in the shower with me. El and pug. When angel saw us he jumped on the floor and curled up. He anticipated the cut but us brothers had another plan. They had nice soaps in socks and started beating him with them

Angel started yelling but i grabbed his mouth and covered them with my hands. Sometimes he would get loose and get out a yell but id cover him again. We did this for about 40 minutes. Some guys would walk by the shower and look throught the doors glass window but they would Keep on moving. When i went to locos cell across the hallway. They said they could hear him and i guess the officer heard too becquse he was closer. Loco was also running a store and i told him that pug wanted a box of donuts two for 1. He had the officer open his door and he Handed me the donuts.

It was christmas 23,96. the goon squad waa coming in the unit. It was about10:00 am. My door opened. They told me to get on my knees and put my hands behind my back. If i did anything else they werw going to pepper spray me.

They took me and my cellmate el and they went in the cell next door and grabbed pug. They took us to segregation. The escorted us one by one into the interrogation area. The luitenant should me pictures of a black and blue all over body. Asked me if I had anything to tell him. I told him no. I was sent back to my single cell in seg. I had a brother in the cell next to me named large. He was like why do they have you good soldiers in seg? I told him that I did not know must be pending investigation. El was in the cell across from me. A ticket was slid trough my door on the side. It said that I assaulted inmate Gonzalez. Pug was on the other side. I could hear him saying masters forever forever masters. I asked him what was up. He said I got my ticket. I asked him what did he want me to do. I told him I could take the weight. He said do it. When the next lutinent came on shift I asked him if I could speak to him. He had me escorted to his office. I told him that I assaulted Gonzalez because he disrespected me in the shower. It was just me and him. He gave me paperwork to fill outand I filled it out. He asked if I was ready to plead out on the ticket and I said yes sir. I signed the guilty plea and he gave me 10 days seg time on the finding. I was then escorted to my cell. A week later my door was popped for me to go to a displinary hearing, they told me that my ticket could not be copped out to that this ticket had to go to the board. But because I pled guilty the finding was guilty. They found pug and el guilty too. We were all shipped out of the facility about two weeks later. We were in seg for 30 days. They sent us to the close custody program at metlow correctional center. There was a hearing and I was found guilty for being a secrurity group threat member. Me and el went to the same block c and pug went to block d. I was placed in the cell with a grand master. His name was tragic. I told him I don't know why pug and el ws there because I terminated Angel all by myself. I showed him a copy of my dispinary report. he was in prison for killing two lord kings on broad street in the daylight they drove up around the corner tragic walked back and blasted both of them walked back to the car and drove off. He never snitched on anyone in the family. he was a stand up guy too after knowing him for awhile. He said he heard of me and wanted to step down. He thought I would be a good grandmaster but I declined his offer. Officer rege would bring in grey market movie for us to watch on his third shift watch. We mostly watched movies played chess and listened to the radio together. He was a good celly. He went to the program in phase 2 before me. When I got there I was placed in the cell with a heartbreaker. He was an asshole. He used to talk about all the violent things hed done in prison and in the street. He was heavily medicated. One afternoon at stand up count he shoved me and told me to get out of his way. I lost it. I turned around and started punching him in the face. He never punched back. the office walked by doing his count and saw me. He said knock it off. I stopped punching him. Reinforcement came and excorted both of us to seg. Captain Simon was the captain for the gang threat member units. He questioned me but I said I didn't have anything to say. I was sent back to my cell in segregation I was in the cell with one of my brothers Stedero. Kyler was on his way back to his cell. Stedero ask me if I did that to him. His whole face was swelled up. I told stedero that I did what I had to do. I didnt feel comfortable around kyler. When the dr ivestigeater came around for a plead to a fighting ticket. I asked him what was kyler in seg for he didn't do anything I swung on him first during and last he never swung back. the dr investigator asked if I was sure and I said yeah. He said one moment he left and came back with another paper. It said assault on it. He asked me how did I plea and I said guilty. He gave me 10 days in seg. i was the the talk of the town when I returned to block c. all anyone wanted to talk about was what I did to that guy. The next 90 days was a breeze. I was in the program again. Hold up there was some familiar faces in there. Wiz was there with Cocky ralph. I heard cocky ralph got terminated in block a but he was still claiming to be a brother. every time I was around him he would say" In Masters we trust". His claim was that the supreme masters that was in the facility were not supposed to be supreme masters accourding to the founder of our organization. I wasn't realy trying to be a politician so I just let it be. There was no positions in the program. The goal was to get to population. Maybe there was no big deal. All of Connecticuts prisons were kind of the same. In close custody by being affiliated to a gang, odds were you were going to be denied for parole. It was 23 hour lock down but altleast I had my television and radio. It was more of a program designed to make someone want out. There was stand up count at 8 am and 4 pm if you were not at at attention you received a class c display report. In phase 2 gang awareness groups were mandatory. AT THE time I had a subscription to porn magazines.

Wiz asked if he could see one one day. I was like sure. No hard feeing. but when he got the mag he said I was beat. I'm a fun guy I don't get mad I get even. The next morning he was coming from breakfast he walked passed my door and saw me. I poured a whole 22 ounce cup of urine on his head. He walked straight and I locked my door. he went straight to the cops and told them what I had done. They told him to take a shower and he did. I was escorted to seg again. This time I was moved to block d there was a lot of ids there. There was a supreme master asking me what happedend in the program. I told him. He said wiz was a real pain. Good for you he said. You wanna be a grand master merlin he asked. He said the kids really needed it. I said sure. He asked me if I was in the family for a year atleast and I told him yeah. He said that was the requirement to hold a position. At first me and him mostly just talked to brothers aout there problems and issues that arose. The other two supreme masters were in seg. They were moved to block d when the got out and all hell was breaking loose. Supreme master fletcher was put in my cell. He was very strict. The other brothers used to always initiate wrestling with me but I would block and mostly push them away. he was always saying to stop playing with them but I said that was my self defense strategy I didn't want to hurt them. He gave the orders through me to bounce them. Everytime a brother would put his hands towards me I would block them and tell them they had to take a 30 second bounce minimum. Those bounces didn't matter to them they were being more agrressive. I ended up steping down. I didn't realy need a position. The next day we dd not get our recreation al day. They blocks lights were turned of and it was like 9 pm. I told fletcher to put his sneakers on because he never knows what gonna happen. I started kicing on the door realy hard. The whole block started making noise now. They were kicking and screaming thoughout the unit. One cop ended up coming to our cell and saying your going to seg to my celly. Flethcher said it wasn't him and then the other cop pointed and said it the other one. I was escorted to seg once again but the cop said I threatened him. Maybe his old ass didn't hear properly nut I cped out to the ticket. when I got ut of seg I was moved back to block c. I was placed In a cell by myself. I went to recreation and everything seemed cool. After about a couple of days another brother came into the unit from block d. I remember him he was about 22 and I was 26 now. We talked about it and he said hed move in my cell, the capt was on vacation but lutinet lander was in bump asked the lutinant if he could move in my cell. The luitinant asked him if he had any problems with me and he said no. that we were col with eachother. He moved in. we used to talk throught the windows with our very own sign language and the supreme masters had decided that I be a supreme master. We were telling block c but they didn't want to hear it. One day I was walking to the shower and some heartbreaker was yelling through the door merlin is gay him and his little buddy swings that way. I asked him what he was talking about and he said askt the correctional officers. I paid him no mind and took my shower. On the way back from the shower one of my other brothers was getting of the shower. He was calling me a child molestor. I went up in his face and told him to watch his fucing mouth. He started shaking and the correctional officers told me to let it go. We went to rec the next day and the same brother tried to bring me up on charges saying that a correctional officer saw me getting my dick sucked by my young celly. I smacked him in the face with a basketball immidaitley. His celly then ran up behind me and hit me in the back of my head. I tilted a little bit. I looked around and my celly was fighting with him. I turned back around a started chasing nick. I knew some of his street homiess and he knew me from the street but we weren't in the same circles. When I caught up to him he tried to bend down a little bit so he could get under me and grab me but I kneed him and the face. He then droppred to the ground and wrapped his arms around my leg I started punching him where I could until staff came. They tried to break it up. I stpped puching him and they got him to stand up. He then trytied to punch me but the cops pepper tazed him we al went to seg. They asked me what cel I wanted to go in 7 or 6 and I tld them 7. They put my same cely in the cell with me and placed them in 6 cell. One of the officers spit on their cell window. I don't reallyknow what was going on. I went back to block d and when asked what happened over there I told them. Fletcher told me he cant allow brothers to be assautig eachother and said the only time you can swring on a brother is in self defense. That's when the other brother swings first. He ordered a 2 minute bounce. My cellmate max bounced me bt he was gentle, one day I was going taking a shower and getting ready for for court when I say my cely that helped me out was going to rec. he said I master u master we master and stepped thru the doors, I went to court for my habeau corpus trail. When I got back officer boseman said that me and my old celly put a hit out on him and that he feared for his life. We got found guilty fro threating and I was sent back to block c. this time the guy that I beat up was grand master. They said they gave him the postion because he needed some respect and he was an old timer. He was a heroin addict plain and simple who made a life out of coming and going to cells over and over again. I was in the cell all alone until I got a new cely who came in from off the streets. At first he was saying he was in prison for domestic violence but when fletcher questioned him he said he was in prison because he got caught with a kilo. I try to be nice to the guy I would share my food with him and let him watch my television. Maybe guys take kindness for weakness. ONE DAY he just kept swinging on me. I picked up my coffee mug and hit him in the face with it. He bent down as to scoop me when I was punching him and I put my thumb in his eye to gouge him. the cops came to the door and told us tho break it up. They told him to put his hands though the trap door. They put handcuffs on his front. They told me to come on and I started walking toward him. I just didt trust the dude so I started punching him in the face. He tried to duck and I uppercut him. Then the cops pepper spayed us through the door. I went back to seg anf then back to block. When I got to block d the rumor was spread by hightower that I tried to rape him. It was a new unit. Most of the trouble makers were transferred to to supermax. There were aot of rumors going around. One rumor was that the cose custody program was being moved to the supermax. I was unsuccessful with my habeus corpus trial accouding to my court appointed attorney. Michelle had testified that I was sleeping at the time of the accident but it did not mean anything. I thought that my next best avenue was parole but there Was a slim possibility due to my gang activity in prison. If I was not receiving my 13 dollar a week donation from masters 360 I probably would have been let it go but I did try parole ad was shot down. They told me even though was a no drug dependant offender I should still go to the drug program the department offered. I signed up for the tier program and went to na aa group. I was going to whatever programs they offered me. The first question they asked me at the tier program was what was my drug of choice. told them coffee. Theother inmates started laughing. The director told me she wanted to talk to me and she pulled me I her office, she asked me if I used drugs and I told her I was a non drug dependant offender. She looked I the computer and that's what it said posseson of narcotics by a non drug dependant offender 15 year sentence. She said that she thought the judge made a mistake. She did not have me return to drug program and she recommended me to the textile factory. I was reclassified to the cloting factory. I learned to sew to clothing there, too bad t wasn't permant because my level was lowerd and I ws transferred to a less secure facity. I went to parole again after two year bt was denied agin. I had another parole date and denied. One night I was working as a volunteer janitor. I had acess to the main hallways at night. I used to wax the kitchen floors and lay down the tables. I had my own store where I was giving 1 for 1 and a half I was real popular there, I met some guys and they were talking or secret language.

They even started controlling other people languages I though. One was david and the other one chris. I started thinking they were government or something. I was watching television and noticed all the logos to te television stations where grey and black. I told the officer I wanted to go cean up the kitchen and he showed me a grey and black pen. I went into the coriders and started paying attention to the numbers. 391 was cia in our supreme alphabets and I started thinking I was never getting out of prison. I didn't know what I was involved in anymore. The address to cybol correctional center was 391 highland aveue. I stood in the hallways for a second thinking and then the doors closed on me. About 1 in the morning staff came around and ask me what I was doing out there. I told them but I was written up for attempted excape. I was sent back to the superax. I was in phase one without a television and word was that you couldn't have atelevision in the supermax anyore. I didn't come out my cell for about 3 months. I was watching up in my sink. I didn't want to be bother. One day the correctional officers cam to my cell and told me I had to take a shower. I did. When I went back in the cell I noticed strange voices coming from my vent. I thought it was my grandmother on an airplane and she was saying merlin come with us. I heard a voice that I remember as this chick name myra and she was getting freaky with me then I heard my cusin micheal saying the myra is a super hoe. The rest of the voices sounde alien to me. One day mental health came to see me and was asking me questions. I never realy paid attention to the questions they asked me. One of the questions was was I hearing voices. I told them yes. They diagnosed with a schitzo affeyctive. i was asked if I wanted medication and I was like no at first but eventually I gaver it a try. Clonazepam and seriquil had me high as kite. I started sleepin alllllloooooot. i refused to do the phase program I was programed out. I was just gonna discharge from the supermax in a year and a half. That what I was thinking but somehow I got transferred a mental health unit inside aother prison I was discharging from there soon, a woman came to my door one afternoon and told me she was going to apply for disability for me from social security. i told her I ddnt want it. She was shaking and she closed my door. Within a few days to discharge my sentence atfter 13years I was asked to submit a dna sample. I told them I wasn't a sex offender vut they said it was for all inmates upon discharge, I refused it saying that WAS NOT A PART OF MY AGGREEMENT IN court. i did not discharge on my date and my mother was worried about me. She tried to contact everyone she could including the governor as far as what was going on with me. I didn't discharge because I caugfht an outside case for refusing the dna. When I was going to court it seemed like things were going on around me I was in a grey truck being transported to court and I could swear that all I saw were grey cars on the highways, I tried to distract myself by looking at the tall building, all our buildings in Connecticut were between 50 and 100 stories tall, those were our homes our businesses our government our churches etc. Farms were normally 4 stories tall. I started hearing voices in my head saying that I am the one. There was a meeting with some people and they testified in court that I was incompentent and could not stands trial and suggested that I go to a state hospital. I hadn't been in touch with anyone on the street I three years not even a phone call or letter. i was at the state hospital for about two years, the case was dismissed but I had to wait for housing. In ct you could not leave the hospital until you had a place to live, I didn't have a place to live, I started thinking about michelle again. The last time I saw her was at a visit in 96. I didn't look at her in her face I would just look down. She said I was smart. I heard she was married to doctor and had kids. It really hurt me. When got out Charlie Aponte was available. He took me shopping and bout me the latest fashion. His son hardcore wasn't in a gang but he did sell drugs, he used to buy from me back in the day. But now I was buying from him and trying to hook p with old people doing old things. I hadn't heard of sage Allen in years seem like no one knew what happened to him. I didn't want to be disrespectful to a church and go there looking for a drug connect. I usualy went with the flow. My social worker found me a room for rent in an apt in east heartford. Thanks to chance and hardcore I was getting aroud again and I was meeting new friends through them hardcore played softball and he was bowling in tornaments. I would often go to the games with him. I didn't have a license or a vehicle but he would pic me up. I didn't need to drive anymore I had chaffuers. Everyone drove me around. I still held my beliefs about drugs. I sold to cops correctional; officers, carpenters business people and even the hearford mayor at one point in time. One day we are drinking in bars the next we are buying marijuana in dispencaries. Maybe one day crack houses will be legal

Printed in the United States
By Bookmasters